Simona Ciraolo

The lines on Nana's Face

Flying Eye Books

London – New York

Today is Nana's birthday! I know she's happy because she likes it when we are all together.

To my wonderful
grandmother Croce.

The Lines on Nana's Face is © Flying Eye Books 2016.

This is a first edition published in 2016 by Flying Eye Books,
an imprint of Nobrow Ltd. 27 Westgate Street, London E8 3RL.

Text and illustrations © Simona Ciraolo 2016.
Simona Ciraolo has asserted her right under the Copyright,
Designs and Patents Act, 1988, to be identified as the Author
and Illustrator of this Work.

Published in the US by Nobrow (US) Inc.
Printed in Latvia on FSC assured paper.

ISBN 978-1-909263-98-7
Order from www.flyingeyebooks.com

But sometimes it looks like she might also
be a bit sad, and a little surprised,
and slightly worried, all at the same time.

So I ask Nana why, and she tells me it might look
that way because of all the lines on her face.

"Do you mind them, Nana?" I ask.

"Not at all," she says. "You see, it is in these lines that I keep all my memories!"

That can't be right. How could there be enough space for a memory in such a small line?

So I put Nana to the test.

"What do you keep here, Nana?"

"Here is that morning, early one spring, when I solved a great mystery."

"And what about this?"

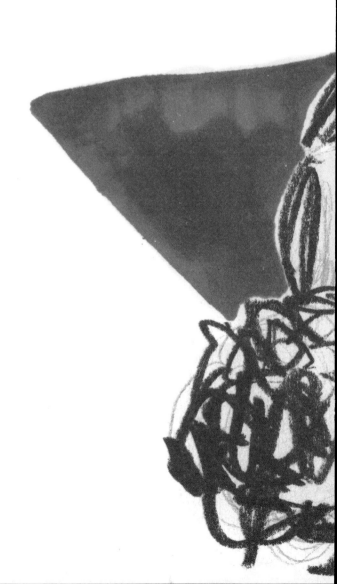

"This is the best picnic I have ever had by the seaside."

"And those?"

"Oh, those are from the night I met your grandpa."

"What's in these little ones?"

"These are from the time I made
my sister the best present ever."

"And what's in there?"

"There is the first time I had to say goodbye."

"Nana! Do you remember the first time you saw me?"

"Yes! That is right here."